I Love You!

written by:
Calee M. Lee

illustrated by:
Tricia Tharp

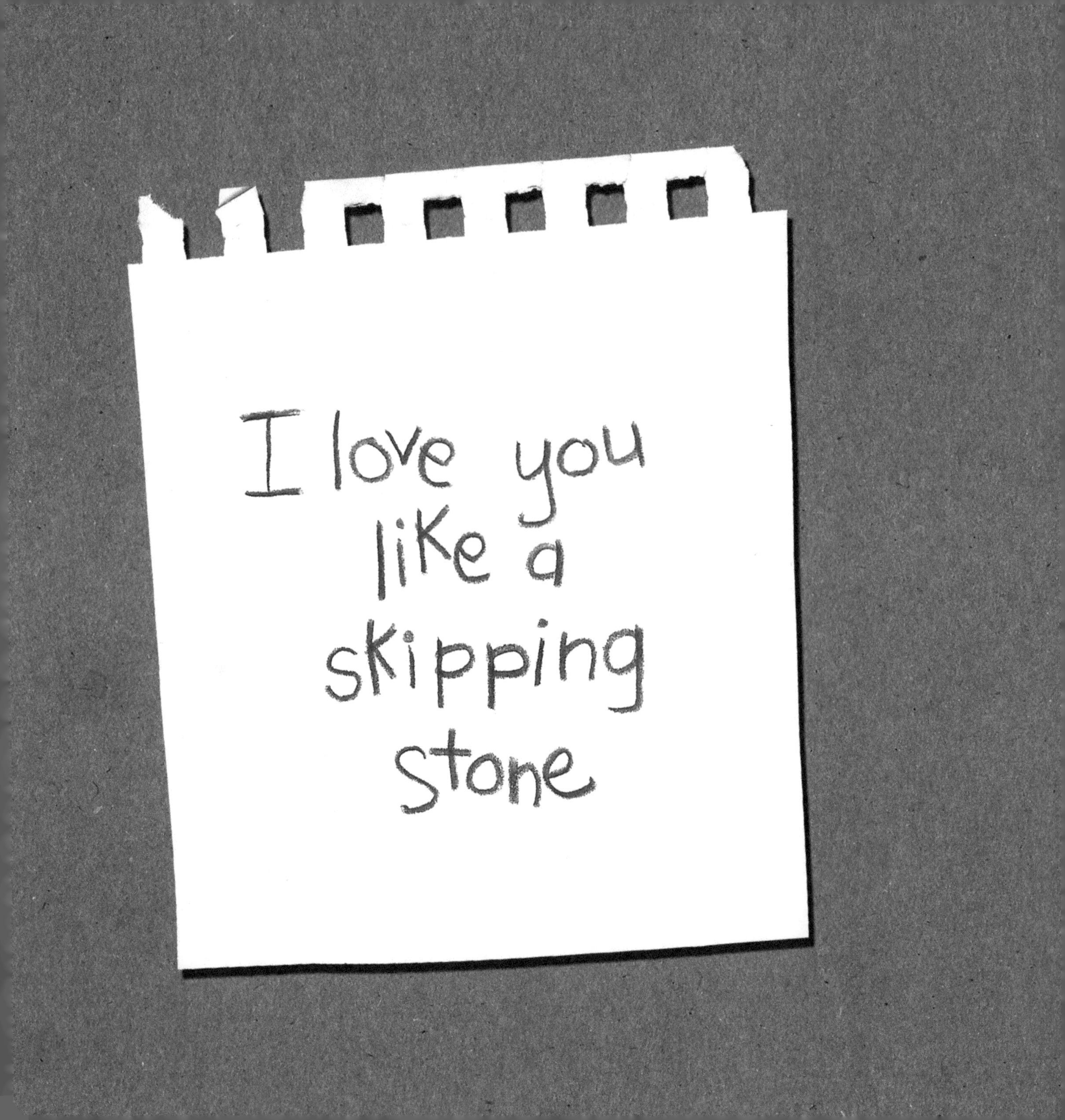
I love you
like a
skipping
stone

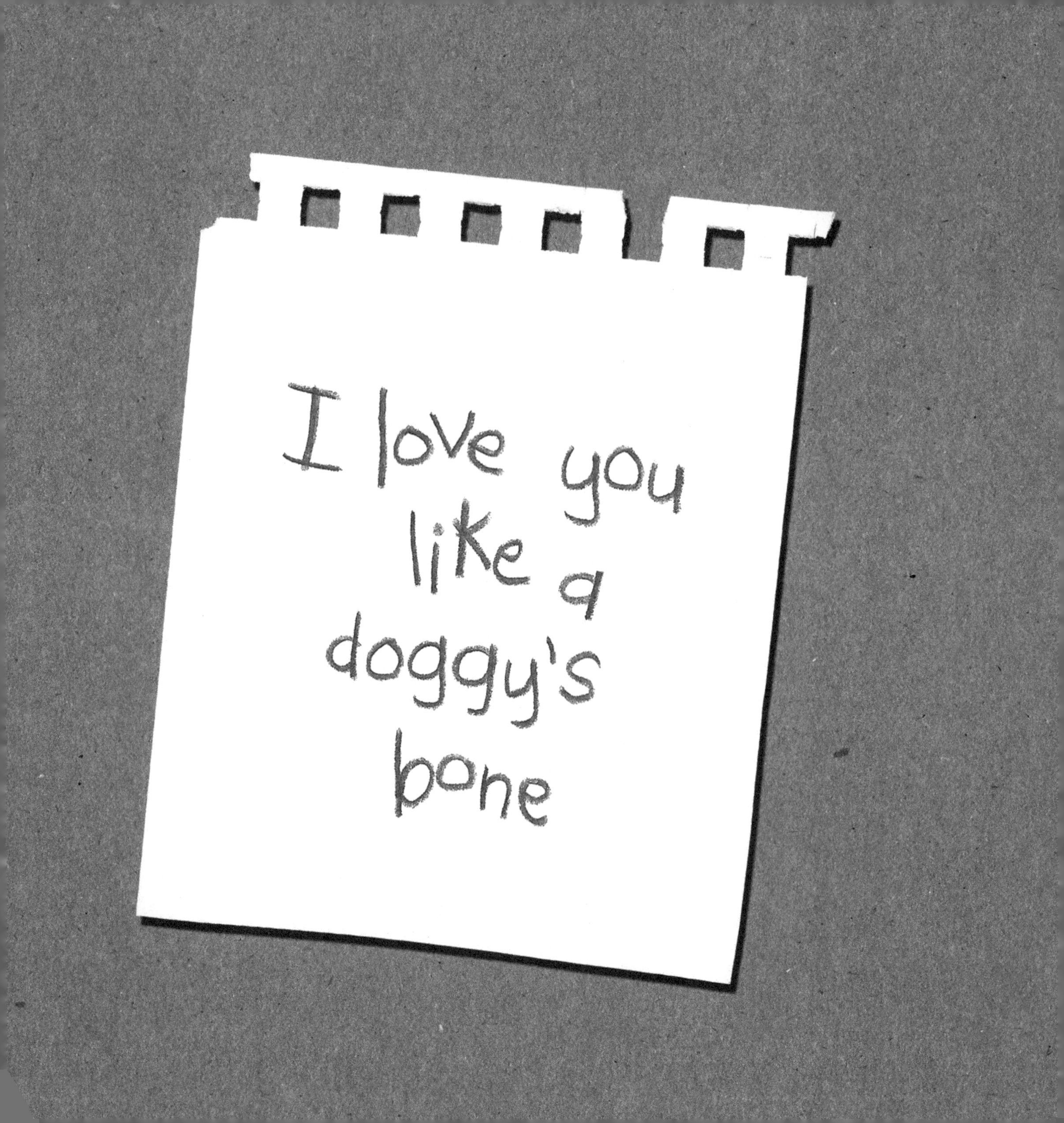
I love you
like a
doggy's
bone

Like the
dizzy after
rolling down
a hill.

I love you
like a
birthday
crown

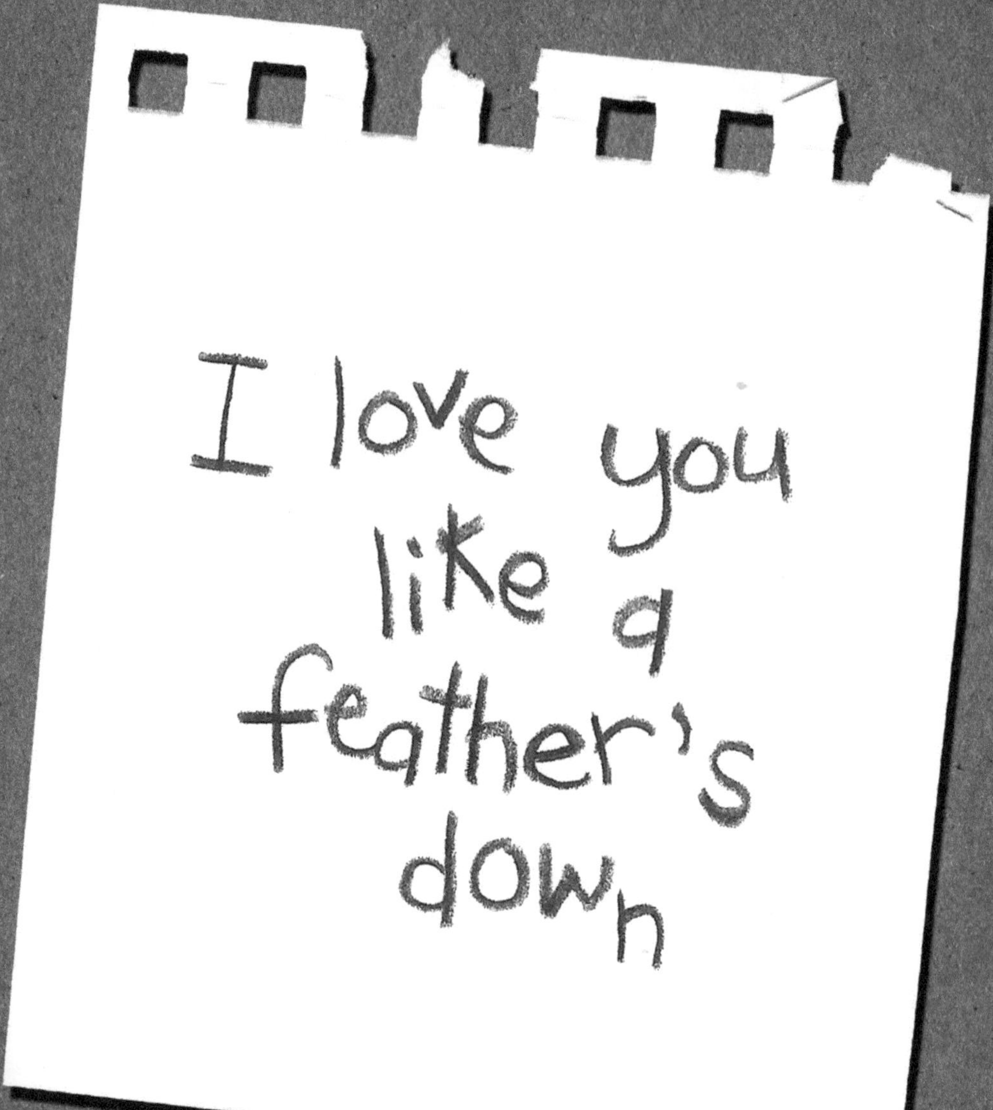
I love you
like a
feather's
down

Like a
lucky coin,
hiding under
a shoe.

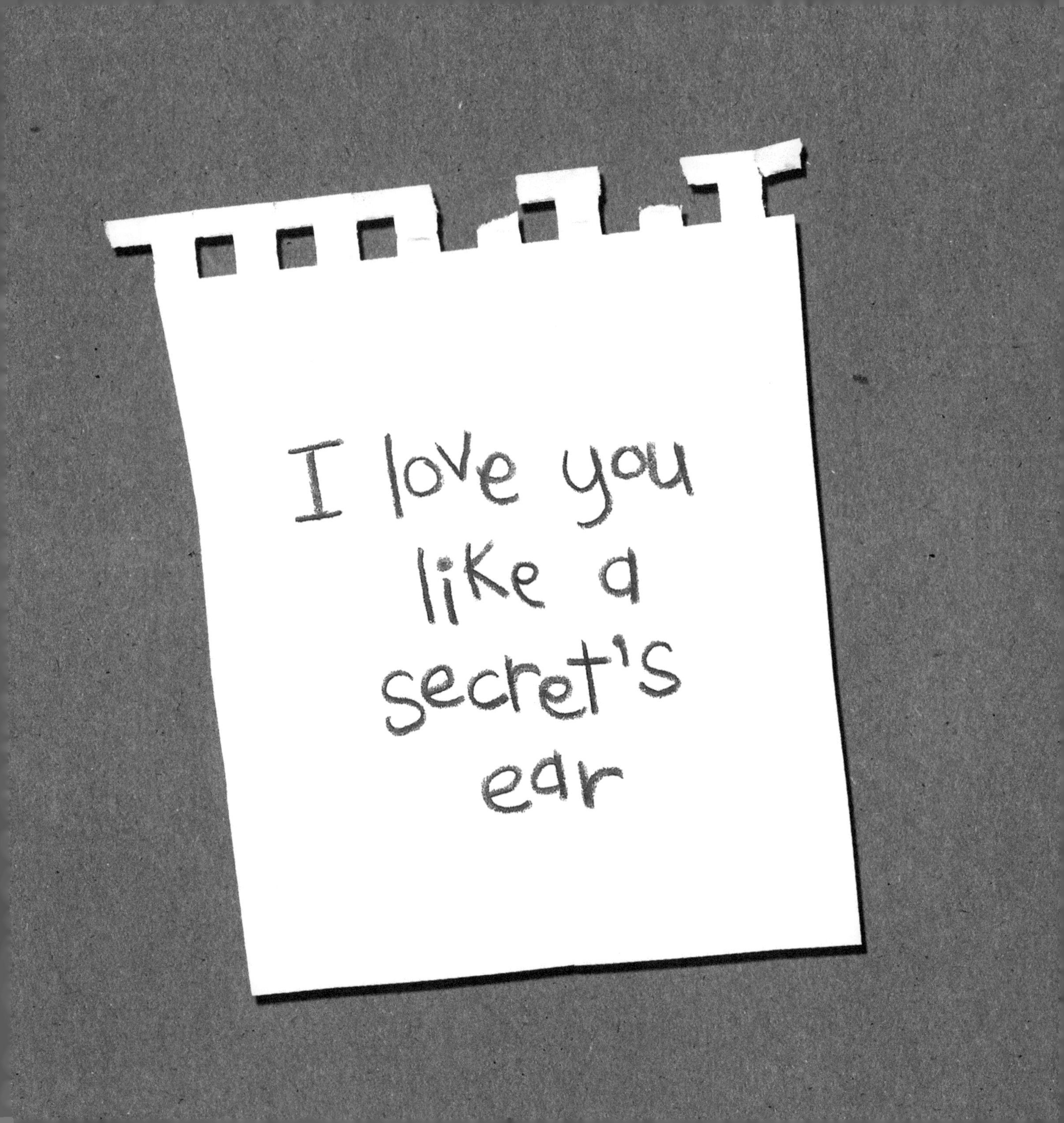
I love you
like a
secret's
ear

Like a
frosty mug
of cold
rootbeer

Like a
pillow fort
that becomes
a magic cave.

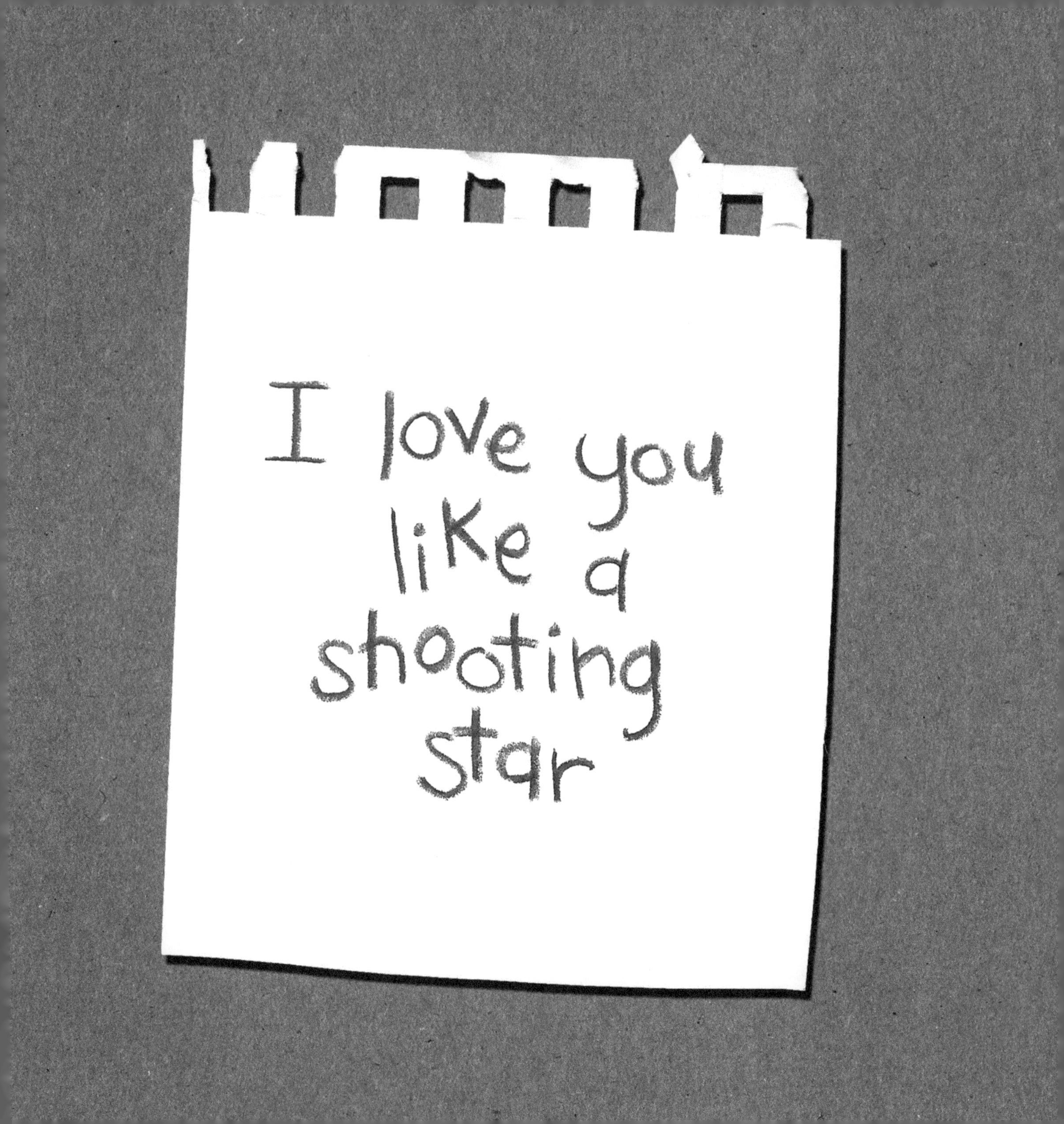
I love you
like a
shooting
star

I love you
like a
skipping
stone

On stage
and when
no one else
can see.

No matter
what
you do
or fear

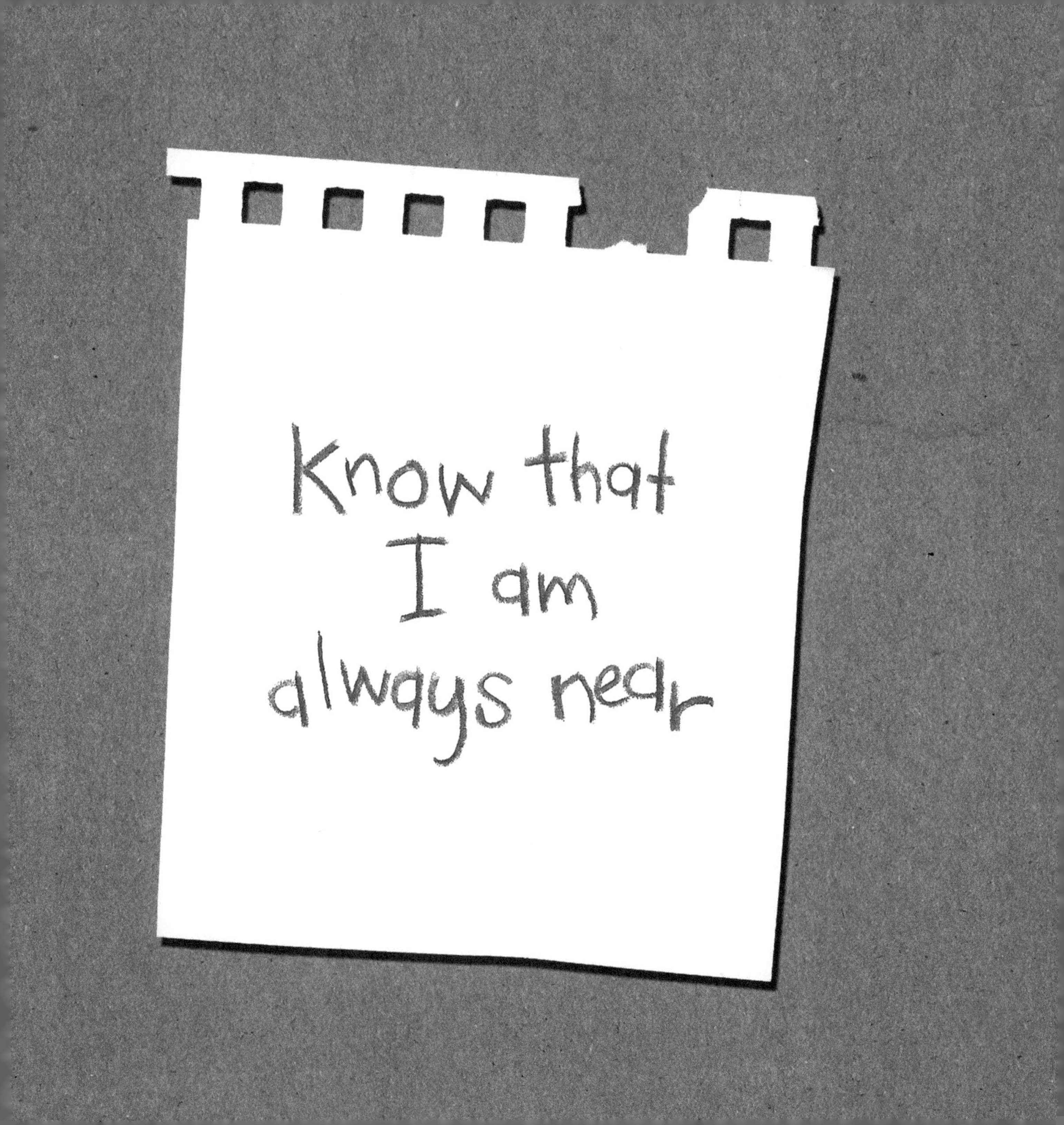
Know that
I am
always near

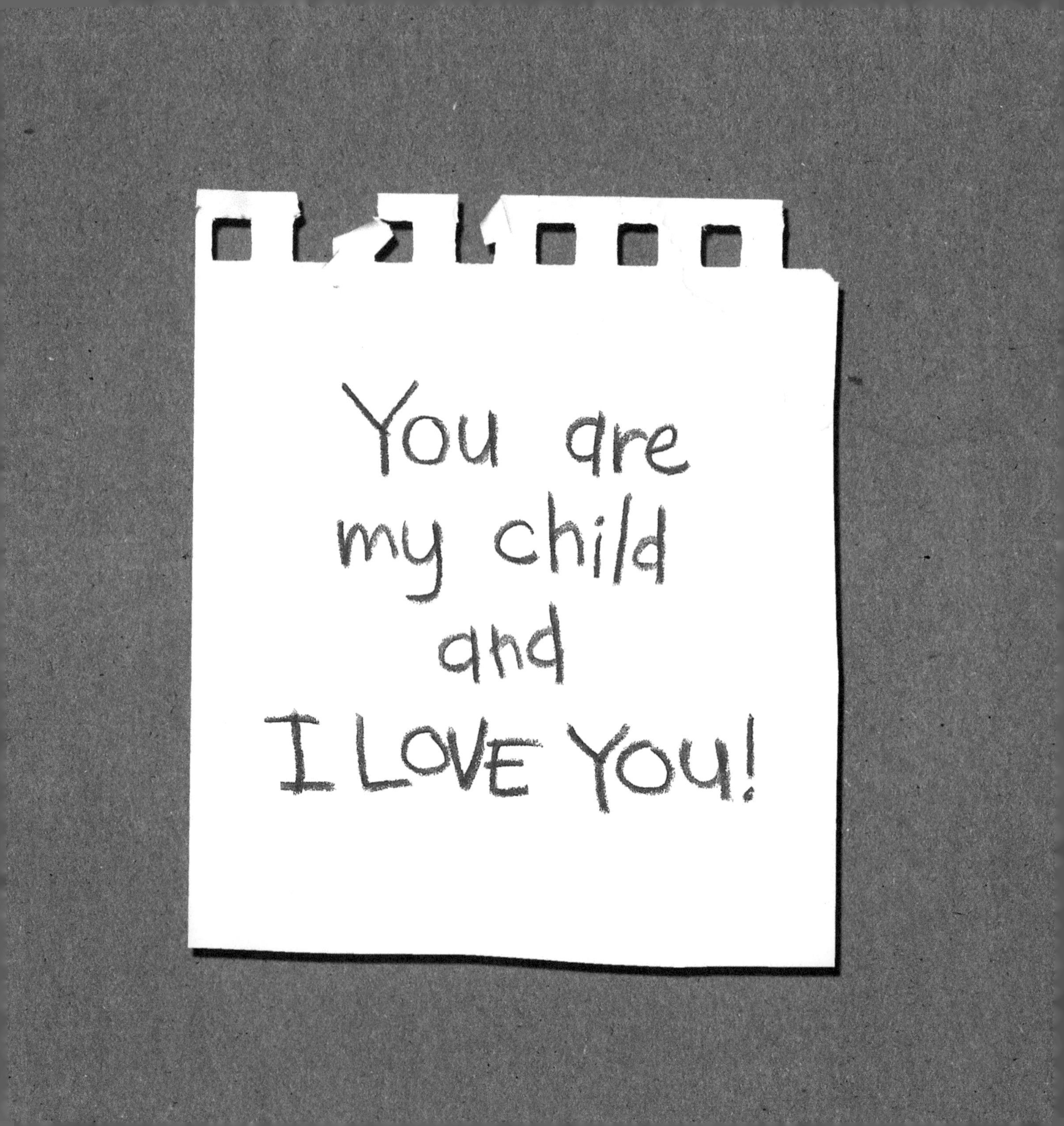
You are
my child
and
I LOVE YOU!

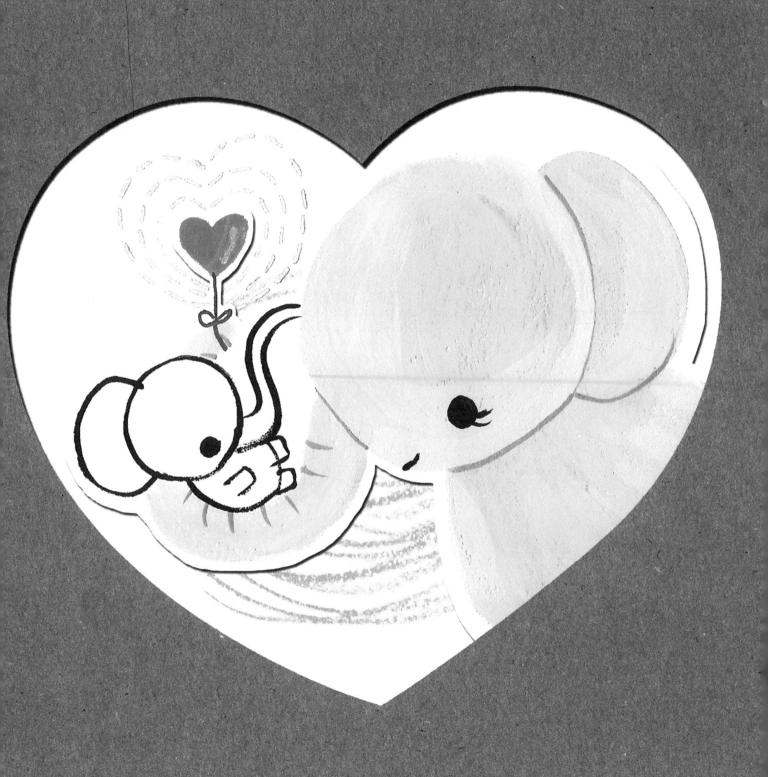

CPSIA information can be obtained
at www.ICGtesting.com
Printed in the USA
BVHW020804040720
582948BV00006B/458

9 781623 954710